bird

bird

angela johnson

DIAL BOOKS | NEW YORK

Published by Dial Books
A member of Penguin Group (USA) Inc.
345 Hudson Street
New York, New York 10014

Designed by Teresa Kietlinski
Text set in Garamond
Printed in the U.S.A. on acid-free paper
10 9 8 7 6 5 4 3 2 1

Library of Congress Cataloging-in-Publication Data
Johnson, Angela, date.
Bird / Angela Johnson.
p. cm.
Summary: Thirteen-year-old Bird follows her stepfather from
Cleveland to Alabama in hopes of convincing him to come home,
and along the way helps two boys cope with their difficulties.
ISBN 0-8037-2847-6
[1. Runaways—Fiction. 2. Stepfathers—Fiction.
3. Interpersonal relations—Fiction. 4. African Americans—Fiction.
5. Alabama—Fiction.] I. Title.
PZ7.J629Bi 2004
[Fic]—dc22
2003022793

for ruth paton

bird

1
bird

IT rained more than I ever saw it rain last night. The sun hadn't gone down yet, so I saw the first part of the storm. The second part I heard beating down on the tin roof of the shed I'm sleeping in.

My feet got wet.

My legs got wet.

Then water poured in overhead faster than it ran under the door. By the time I could see the lights of the farmhouse across the field shining in the dark, I was soaked. All I could think about was when I'd be dry again. I didn't think I ever would be. I even started to think I probably never had been dry or happy anytime in my whole life. Being cold and wet can sure make you feel older than thirteen.

I was feeling really old.

And I was missing just about everybody I knew in the world.

Never have seen this much rain in my whole life.

I never thought it would be this way. I thought it was enough to be so sad and not want to be home anymore. I thought it was enough that I had to lose two fathers before I'm even a teenager.

Cecil's gone, but I have this feeling I can get him to come back, though Mom says he's gone forever. She says he probably never even looked back. I think maybe he did. Maybe.

My mom gave up easy.

I remember her yelling at Cecil about how mad she was that he could have a whole other set of people in his life we didn't know about.

She never used to give up that easy. Once she drove to almost every store in Cleveland looking for a doll that I wanted. She could have called, but she said sometimes people didn't go the extra mile on the phone. I didn't know exactly what that meant, but I got the doll.

I guess in the end I'm more like my mom than I thought. 'Cause I've gone a lot of miles.

Never have seen this much rain in my whole life.

I used to stare in store windows and dream about how I would look in this or that dress. Maybe it would float around me like butterfly wings, see-through, with lots of colors. Or maybe it would sway and swirl the way my sister Lita's wedding dress did the day she got married to Jake. (Except I'd want mine not to end up with cocktail sauce all down the front of it 'cause my cousin Earl thought it was funny to throw shrimp during the Electric Slide.)

I was the flower girl and that night everybody said I looked just like my dad. So when I got home, I held the framed picture of me and him sitting on a swing together.

I do look like him. But I don't remember him,

except for one thing. He used to chase me all over the backyard. We'd run and laugh, fall down and run some more. I used to love running away from him and having him catch me.

Yesterday's storm seems so far away, but now I'm glancing down at myself and I know I look real scary and not like my dad at all. I just got a look at myself for a few seconds in the back-door window of the farmhouse. I think the whole family has gone to church because today might be Sunday. I'm losing days.

The sun had only been up a couple of hours when they all came out of the house looking neat and shiny. Then they got into the station wagon instead of the pickup.

They all looked so happy, while I was picking bugs off the lime green sweater that I used to like so much.

But that's all okay 'cause now I can eat.

Sundays are always the best breakfast times.

Pancakes and sausage. The house people have a real picky son who only eats peanut butter sandwiches. I pretty much have whole meals when he's done. They never lock the back door.

I wonder why they trust people so much.

Cecil always said you shouldn't trust anybody. Once I told him I trusted him and Mom, but he just laughed.

I've been eating off their unfinished breakfasts for about three weeks now and they don't even notice it. They don't notice that somebody's been in their house either.

I am somebody else when I'm in their house.

I am not the wild-hairdo girl who ran so far away from everybody she knew. I am not the hungry girl who sneaks food out of strange people's houses and hides during the day, but prowls around at night (even though she's afraid of the dark). I am somebody else when the farmhouse family has gone away.

I am the girl who walks across the creaky hardwood floors that shine like puddles in the sunshine, and lies across the soft couch with the quilt thrown on it. I make sure to say hi to all the family pictures, and

I laugh at how the farmhouse daddy always wears big hats and turns his head weird.

I'm also the girl who sticks her feet in the bathtub and scrubs up as good as she can as fast as she can. But that's going to change today. Today I'm going to take a whole bath, bubbles and all, in the farmhouse family's nice white tub.

Everything that's wood shines in the living room and smells like lemon polish. I can see my reflection in all the furniture. Mom makes our furniture shine like this. She'd smile into her reflection sometimes and would hold the polish up to me like she was interviewing me for a TV show.

More reason for a bath: Water makes me happy when I'm sad and thinking about Mom.

I walk up the stairs, running my hand along the nice white walls and looking at all the family pictures that hang along the staircase. Everybody in this farm family smiles.

Even the people in the old black-and-white pictures smile.

My people don't smile.

We never took a family picture. Can't imagine it. I don't think my mom and Cecil, my stepfather, could stand being in a small room together for that long. Cecil had to leave Lita's wedding reception. He said he'd spent enough time with family. Mom threw a roll at his back as he walked out the door.

But this family is different.

It will be magic to bathe in this nice family's house.

The top step creaks as I walk down the hall to the bathroom. I have to hold myself back from going to the farm girl's bedroom with its stuffed animals and yellow and lavender flowered quilt and posters on the wall. It's where I usually spend my early Sunday mornings.

But not this time.

I go into the blue-tiled bathroom with the sparkly white floor and all the shiny faucets. I lean down and smell the big white towels all rolled up in a basket by the window.

They really do smell of spring, like the television says. I breathe it in till I can't anymore.

I breathe it all in.

Then I start running the water in the tub that's got feet at the bottom. Seems like it might take off and run down the stairs any minute. Imagine that out in the field.

There are bottles and bottles of bubble bath and bath salts, bath beads, bath oils, and bath creams. I don't know which to use, so I put a little bit of everything in the running water. The room smells good and steamy as I peel off my jeans and sweater.

I'll wash everything in the tub when my bath is done, then throw it all in the dryer. The farm family is always gone exactly three hours and forty-five minutes on Sunday. I've used up twenty minutes eating and looking.

I made sure I turned on more hot than cold water, and it feels so good when I sink deeper and deeper into the bubbles. It's like I'm in a warm wet flower garden. I close my eyes and try to forget about everything.

The old shed I'm staying in.

The bus that brought me here.

The way the front-door window broke when Cecil slammed it a week before he left.

The feeling I got, when I opened his good-bye gift, that he hadn't really been there at all.

In the tub with feet, I can almost forget about it all.

Cecil used to wake me up at about five o'clock in the morning to go out and run with him. He said he couldn't think of anybody else in the world who didn't mind getting up that early and had the energy of a hummingbird.

I guess that's why he always called me Bird.

When he left, I began thinking that nobody else would ever call me that again, and my heart started to hurt. I remember that I sat out on the stoop and watched people go by for hours and hours without seeing any of their faces. I sat there till the sun started to go down and Mom finally came out and said, "He's not coming back, so you might as well come on in and get on with it."

I did get on with it.

I brushed my teeth, went to school, did my

chores, and held my heart 'cause most times it felt like it was surely falling right out of my chest. Everything in me missed Cecil. Everything. Mom knew it too, and she watched me like I might fall down stairs or break stuff accidentally.

I never got so much attention.

We played Scrabble and shopped. We ate out all the time and even went to the arcade together. Sometimes on her lunch break, she'd get me out of school and we'd sit in Public Square eating Italian sausages and greasy fries and watching all the pigeons. I love pigeons, but Mom, who hates them, never complained.

Things kept going on like that, like one big vacation. Until the dream.

I'm standing in a field in my dream, and I can't see a house or anything else around me. I get dizzy 'cause I keep turning around trying to find something or somebody out there. Finally I give up and just stare across the field.

Then I look down and I'm standing in red dirt and red ants.

Cecil used to talk about the red ants. They bite. He said they'd eat you alive if they could. But in the dream they aren't biting me. There's just thousands of them moving across the field, and something telling me to follow them.

That's what made me leave. Those ants. Everything, nothing, and those red ants.

I don't think I've ever been so clean in my life.

Back in Cleveland I only took showers. Never wanted baths. It took too much time to run all that water and wait for the bubbles and everything. I never had the time. Now the only thing that I want to do is spend the rest of the summer in the farmhouse people's tub. I never want to leave.

It wasn't that hard to get on the bus, 'cause I paid this homeless man to buy my ticket. But when it came time for him to give it to me, he got this concerned parent look on his face.

"Are you okay, child?" he asked.

I said, "Just fine."

"Where do your folks live?"

I lied. "Alabama."

"Why isn't somebody here with you?"

I lied again. "I've been visiting my grandma, but she's sick. She put me in a cab to the bus station. She told me to find a nice older person to buy my ticket, so I wouldn't have any problems."

He knew I was lying, but I think he felt bad for me. I guess he thought I was running away from something pretty awful. And anyway, why would I pick Mobile if I didn't have any relatives there?

He handed me my ticket, shook his head, and took a can of pop out of his coat. "Do you want a cold drink, young lady?"

"No, thank you," I said.

When I really looked at him, I realized he wasn't as old as I first thought he was. As a matter of fact, I think that the guy couldn't have been past thirty, only he looked tired and run-down. But he was nice to me.

He told me things.

Don't talk to people. Tell anybody who asks that

my father is meeting me, but don't tell them in what city.

Always sit close to the bus driver, and only get out when there isn't any other choice or I have to change buses. Always sit in the aisle seat.

I nodded my head to everything and even smiled when he said that I should call home, no matter what.

When the bus pulled off of Prospect Avenue, he waved to me. He was the last person I spoke to in Cleveland before the bus bumped onto the highway and I was on my way to look for Cecil.

I make sure the bathtub is sparkling after I drain all the water out. I dry all around the floor and tub. I take my wet towels and throw them in the dryer by the back door with all of my clothes. Wrapped in the farm girl's robe, I wait on the living room couch for everything to dry.

The slamming of a car door wakes me up. At first I don't know where I am, but can think clear enough to run to the back door, take the robe off, and get into my clothes. I put the robe in the dryer with the towels, then hurry out the back door to the field and into the woods to spend the rest of my Sunday by the creek.

Later I go back to the field to watch the family.

They sit in the backyard talking and laughing. It's okay for them 'cause I was never there. I didn't mess up their Sunday.

I'm clean.

Not so hungry now.

Not so tired.

And I wonder what the farmhouse people would do if I just walked up to them and said, "Hey."

Would they invite me to dinner, ask me where I came from and how long I'm going to stay? Would they let me share their daughter's yellow and lavender room and run out all the hot water for a bubble bath? Would they give me a big old plate of pancakes and sausage all my own? Would they tell me about the relatives in the pictures in their lemon-smelling house?

By the time I've settled down in the shed across the field from the good farm people's house, I decide that they would do all of that and more if I walked on up to them.

I had the dream about the red ants again and decided in the morning that maybe next Sunday I might just be waiting for the family on their porch when they got back from church.

Maybe.

2
ethan

THE moon woke me up a minute ago.

It always does. Doesn't have to make a noise or have to spill anything down from the sky. Just shine in my window and dance shadows off my walls.

It could be the heat too. Maybe the moon shining on me is just enough to push me to very warm and wake me up. April to October it can be real hot here, but my daddy doesn't trust air-conditioning. He says he doesn't trust anything that changes the temperature if he can't see how.

When Mama says what about the furnace, he says that it's wood-burning and he knows all about wood.

"Uh-huh." Mama always laughs.

But what's important now is that I get to watch the full moon and the girl out in the field dancing around underneath it. She dances like she's swimming underwater. Or like she doesn't have any bones or muscles to fight with while she's moving around.

And I'm wondering if she's the girl. The runaway girl Mama asked me if I'd seen.

I said no to Mama.

She didn't tell me anything about the girl except somebody called the house looking for her.

If this girl's not careful, she'll trample on Mama's snap peas, and Mama will think that I've been running through the garden again. But she probably wouldn't be too mad about it anyway. She doesn't get mad. I don't remember her ever yelling at me.

Ever.

My sister Nonie says it's because I was real sick as a baby and the family didn't know if I'd make it.

But I don't think that's why Mama doesn't yell.

Mama picks wildflowers and nurses baby squirrels and raccoons she finds in the woods. She smells sweet like magnolia and never blows the car horn. Daddy talks softer when she's in the room.

The world whispers when Mama is near.

I'm thinking now that the girl dancing under the moon might make the world whisper too.

Every time we go to the grocery store lately, it's all I can do not to say: "Mama, you need to get that strawberry syrup, 'cause that girl who lives in the shed likes that kind on her pancakes."

Mama always worries that I don't eat enough. Anytime I ask for food, day or night, she shovels it right at me.

So instead I say, "I like that strawberry syrup and I think we need more . . ."

We have a lot of strawberry syrup. I don't want us to run out. If we do, the shed girl might decide to go away for good. She might decide to dance off down the road and out of the county like she dances under the moon.

I worry about the shed girl, so I've been leaving bags of apples and things around. I'm starting to wonder if she thinks it's strange that food keeps showing up all around her. Fruit, potato chips, pies, baked chicken . . .

When I was real little, I used to think everybody had nurses and doctors and lab people around them every day. I thought all kids stayed in the hospital for months at a time, wore pajamas everywhere, and knew all the secret, cool, alcohol-smelling rooms that nurses told you with big smiles and hands on their hips to stay out of.

By the time I was three, I knew how to reset my own IV and just what part of my arm would be right to take blood out of for tests.

I knew when the treatments were working and when they weren't. I could tell if it was a weekday or weekend in the hospital by what color Jell-O we got at lunch.

And sometimes, when everybody was gone, I could hear my heart pumping and the blood running through my whole body. It was these times that I felt like a clock. Tick tock.

I didn't get much time alone because my family visited me in the hospital so often. Mama was there every day. I saw my brother David and sister Nonie mostly on the weekends, and Daddy whenever he could get away from work.

He'd come to the door of my room and it would be the same thing every time.

"How's it going, kid?"

"Okay, I guess."

"You guess?"

"Yep, Daddy; I guess."

"You mean you don't know?"

"I guess not."

"Do you mean yes, or no, or you don't know?"

By then I'd be giggling so much that I'd have to hide my face under the covers for a while to stop laughing, because Daddy's face would be so serious. His shoulders would start shaking, though, and he'd be laughing too.

But the part I couldn't wait for was when he'd

walk over to me, past the IV and all the other monitors, and pick me up so soft that the whole world got still and quiet.

Then too I could hear my heart beating. Then it was just the quiet, Daddy, and my heart.

They had an ox roast after church last Sunday and we were supposed to go, but Mama changed her mind. She was talking to this woman with a boy about my age, then got a funny look on her face and ran to Daddy. A few minutes later we were on our way back home like usual.

I hoped the shed girl got enough to eat while we were at church.

If I could run really fast, I'd run across the field and down into the woods to the place where the shed girl spends most of her time.

I'd climb a tree and sit up in it all day long and watch her hop through the pond and catch frogs that she holds for a little, then lets go. She never keeps them for pets. You'd think she would. She must get lonely.

Her eyes look lonely. But maybe I just imagine

them that way. I've never gotten that close to her. She almost fell over me, though, one day by the old willow near the creek.

I was there before her. Waiting. She showed up and wham! She was about five steps from me and she was pulling that green sweater of hers over her head to go for a swim.

By the time she'd hit the water, I was halfway back home.

My chest hurt and I was sweating. I could hear the blood in my head. And when I looked down, my feet were running. But I was still alive. Alive.

Always thought if I ran too hard, it would be the end of me. But it wasn't. My new heart pounded, then slowed down to a regular beat just as I walked into the backyard.

Mama was in the hammock singing a song she always sang there or when she was in the old rocking chair on the front porch. A song that makes me think of warm blankets and how good it feels when you come in out of the cold. I moved closer.

Then I watched her fall asleep. I took the iced tea

out of her hand, drank the rest, and fell asleep on the soft grass underneath the hammock and dreamed of running, willow trees, and girls in green sweaters dancing beneath them.

3

jay

STUFF happens all the time and usually there's nothing you can do about it. The other times you watch it happen and don't do the right thing to stop it.

That's what it's like, my pop always says. And once when I asked him what "it" was, he just smiled and kept on walking down the path to the creek. We finally sat down by the water and he said, like he'd been talking the whole time, "Living day to day."

Yeah, living day to day, stuff happens all the time and there's not too much you can do about it. Like the morning I hollered at my brother because he'd taken a video game out of my side of the room.

"Put it back!" I yelled.

"Make me!" he screamed louder, then he jumped on the bus and laughed because he knew I'd never find the game on his messy side.

Nine hours later I was in the waiting room at the hospital thinking about how when we got home I'd let him have the game anyway. Suddenly Pop was standing over me and we were all falling, lost, into a thousand-acre wood.

I see the boy at church running sometimes and I can remember when he could barely take two steps without wheezing and bending over. They had to start bringing him in a wheelchair.

He laughs now. A lot.

He runs down the church stairs and even jumps into the back of his parents' station wagon to drag out a picnic basket. A couple of weeks ago I even saw him kicking a soccer ball around the church yard.

I read somewhere that when people get other folks'

hearts, they wake up craving things to eat they never liked much before or sometimes had never tasted.

I wonder if this boy likes peanut butter. That's all my brother Derek would eat, peanut butter, to make you sick, he'd eat so much. He used to put it on everything.

Fruit, meats, and vegetables.

Nasty, but that was what he liked. I wish I could watch him eat peanut butter on anything again.

Maybe this kid has Derek's memories even though a brain aneurysm killed him. I guess it doesn't matter.

I still turn over in the night and look at his bed. Left everything just like it was the day he left and never came back. I trip over basketballs, games, and clothes every day, but I won't let my mom pick anything up. I caught her in the room one day eyeing the clothes. I pitched a fit until she just backed out of the room and started to cry.

I think she thought that as the mom, she was supposed to clean it all up.

She doesn't have to.

Nobody does. At least not right now they don't.

Maybe one day I will. Maybe.

But for now everything can stay just like Derek left it because most everyplace else in the house is wiped clean of him. Mom started scrubbing two days after the funeral and only stopped when Pop had to bandage her bleeding hands.

I acted like I didn't see them sitting there on the couch with the bandages and tube of ointment that he was rubbing on her hands.

Most times these days I pretty much try not to notice anything. It's easier that way. I don't want to have to ask anyone how they are because I've been asked that question so much the last year that I almost can't stand being around people anymore.

I'm happy to just sit in front of my computer. And when I'm not doing that I read. I read anywhere.

I kind of figured I was on my own the day I brought a book to the dinner table and neither Mom nor Pop said anything.

Even my brother Ben, who'd taken a semester off college, didn't say anything when I propped the big science fiction book up on the table in front of my plate of spaghetti and meatballs. He always used to be on this thing about having "conversation" at dinner. But he doesn't really talk that much either anymore. I know he can't wait to go back to school and leave this sad old house and the sad people in it.

I've started walking the tracks. Not really going anywhere, but getting far enough away from home that it takes an hour to get back.

My best friend, Googy, throws rocks into the woods off the tracks and listens to hear if she's hit a tree.

She whines, "Man, are we going to just walk these tracks again today?"

"Uh-huh."

"We need a car," she says, picking up a handful of rocks and hitting a trellis overhead.

"Googy, we're fourteen. We don't have our licenses. If we had a car, we wouldn't be able to drive it."

"You just look stupid, right?"

"What?"

She hops off the tracks and jumps up, catches a branch on an old pine, and breaks it off.

"We don't need a license. We could borrow somebody's car and get it back before they know it's gone."

"You mean steal it?"

I look at Googy, who's dressed just like me: baggy shorts, big shirt, tennis shoes. She's wearing sunglasses and a hat, so I can't see her face. I usually know when she's crackin' or just saying something to hear herself speak.

Googy and me got to be best friends when we were both sent to the principal's office in kindergarten for drinking all the chocolate milks for the class lunches. We hid in the kindergarten bathrooms and drank milk till we were both sick.

I threw up in the office.

In sympathy, Googy threw up on the principal. Everybody said we'd been punished enough. Mom and Pop had both laughed at me.

I haven't seen them laugh in months.

❀

I used to mow old Mrs. Pritchard's lawn when I was eight. She had one of those old mowers that was hard as anything to push through all the grass in her backyard. She said she didn't like the gas mowers because they stunk and scared all the birds away.

I wouldn't have done it for anybody else, but she always had lemonade out for me, then she'd feed me the best peach cobbler I ever tasted. I didn't tell her, but I'd have mowed that big yard for nothing but some of that cobbler. I'm easy that way.

It's six years later now, and there isn't any lemonade or peach cobbler on her old front porch.

Now it's just me and Googy sneaking into her garage to steal the old pickup truck that's been sitting there since she had to put Mr. Pritchard in a nursing home.

"Her son comes over and starts it up once a week," Googy says as we look in the garage door windows. "But he's probably just checking on his mom, because Mrs. Pritchard can drive."

The big yellow house is quiet. Mrs. Pritchard is

like a clock and takes a nap every day at eleven in the morning. I remember that she'd sleep for two hours, then come out and sit on the porch.

So we have time.

"The keys should be in the ignition, Jay."

"How do you know?" I ask, wondering how long my idiot buddy's been planning this. Then I start wondering what's wrong with me to be helping her.

I've heard my folks say that if people took the time to think about the dumb things they might do when they're about to do them, they wouldn't.

My folks are wrong.

I've been thinking about this dumb thing for an hour, but I'm still doing it with my just-as-dumb friend.

We don't make a noise opening the garage. It's cool and dark inside. Spotless too. The only thing in it is the pickup and not one bit of dirt.

The truck catches the sun coming in through the garage door. Mrs. Pritchard once told me her husband got the truck when he came home from World

War II. It's old like them. The black paint is perfect and the seats in it look new, but they aren't.

Mr. Pritchard must have loved this truck even more than he did Mrs. Pritchard—but probably only a little bit more, because all the pictures I ever saw of them in the cool doily-covered living room showed them always holding hands and smiling.

Googy and me slip into the truck.

She starts it up and we back out of the garage going real slow. The engine is quiet. We don't make a noise as we pull out onto the street. There's nobody in sight. And since this old neighborhood is at the end of town, we can head to the back roads without anybody even seeing us.

I know I'm a thief, but I don't feel like one.

There's still some roads they haven't paved out in the country, but those are the ones Googy decides she wants to drive.

I hold on to the dashboard because we're flying and the windows are open.

"I thought we were going to take the truck back

like it was when we first borrowed it."

"We will," she screams over some weird opera music she's found on the radio.

"Hey man, it's gonna be covered in red dirt. That's hell to clean."

"It won't be so bad," she says, and keeps on driving.

Googy's a good driver. She's going a little fast, but she takes the curves real careful and doesn't pass other cars or play while she's driving.

Aside from the fact that she's fourteen, a car thief like me, and we're probably gonna get caught and not be allowed to drive till we're about forty—I'd give her a license.

I put my head out the window and watch the fields blowing past. Everything's brown and burnt from the summer sun. The fields of cotton are being plucked clean by the machines.

Everything's all gone.

Even the first summer without my brother is almost gone. We'll all go back to school and start again like he never happened. I'll get on the bus, laugh with people, and go on.

Only I'm stuck because even this ride isn't making me forget about the boy at church running around with my brother's heart in his chest.

He's running around probably eating peanut butter and afraid of spiders like Derek was. Does he like storms and always put one of his feet out from under the covers at night? Does he cheat at cards, or sit real close to his brother or sister during a scary movie?

Maybe his heart is searching for and not finding the place it used to live. I understand that because mine is searching and not finding too.

4
bird

I LIKE the way the red dirt flies way up high on the road, then covers everything with a fine dusting. It's like when you accidentally knock baby powder off the shelf and it goes all over everything. Some things get a lot of it. Other things just barely get touched the farther away they are.

I'm far away and only get a real little bit of the dirt on me. But that little bit makes my hair look brown instead of black. It makes my skin look rusty brown and dry.

Sometimes I feel like I have a whole lot of dirt on

me from being out here as long as I have. Sometimes I just want to sink up to my neck in the pond all day.

It reminds me of the time my mom and her friends went to a health ranch and took pictures of each other in a mud pit. I try not to think about Mom and good stuff.

Mom and shopping.

Mom and the way she laughs.

Mom and the way she puts lipstick on.

In the pond, I sink deeper and move away from the bank. 'Cause I tried it the other day and got leeches on me. All over me and so many, I think I'll have bad dreams for a real long time.

Cecil used to say dreams couldn't hurt me, so he'd never get up when I had a real bad one. I try not to be afraid of the leeches. But leeches are sneaky and you don't feel them at all when you're in the water. They don't sting like bees or pinch like mantises. You're just floating real slow in the water, minding your own business, and bam! All over you. Everywhere.

Anyway, it's funny that the girl driving the truck is really behind the wheel flying down the road. I thought I saw her a few days ago coming out of the grocery and getting on a bike. Didn't look old enough to drive then and probably won't be for a couple of years.

But maybe they just drive real young down here. Or maybe she's sixteen.

Even if she isn't, I like the truck she's driving. Makes me want to drive down these old roads. I feel kind of stuck down here, though. It's getting harder to hide and harder to get out onto the road and get away.

I hope nobody tells on me. But if someone does, I don't think it would be the boy from the farm family—even though I know he sees me. He sees me all the time now. He's scared to come over and say hi and I'm scared to go over and say thanks for not telling your parents I'm living out here in your shed.

We get along. That's the way it is.

Lately I been missing my bedroom.

And pizza. I been missing my bedroom, pizza, and going to the movies with my friends.

I know I missed Christie's birthday party. We planned the party for a whole year. If Cecil hadn't left, I'd have been there like I was supposed to be.

I would have been getting my face painted and tattoos (we all wanted real ones, but Christie's mom laughed so hard at that, we just gave up before we started). I would have been eating chips and birthday cake until I wanted to throw up like every year. I'd have been with everybody.

I wouldn't be alone like I am now.

I wouldn't be lonely.

Never had to be lonely before. I'm not good at it. I'm talking to cows and sheep out in fields now. They listen at least, and you don't have to worry about them calling the cops on you.

Sometimes I go into town for a little bit. It's easy right now, being summer and all. In the summer, you can be somebody's cousin from Michigan or be waiting for your parents who just went into the Fast & Sure Mart for some paper plates or something. You can be almost anybody in the summer.

Just passing through in the summer is good.

The season's going to change, though, and I'm not going to be the passing-through girl much longer. Just like most places, I guess it's got to get colder here in the fall.

My shed won't be enough.

So, I'm going to have to find a warmer place to stay for a longer time.

But mostly now I'm just dreaming about pizza and sometimes, just sometimes, thinking about my mom and how I hope she isn't too worried. I've sent her some letters to tell her I'm fine.

I hope she believes them, 'cause I am. Just fine, I mean.

I hope she isn't dreaming about me in her sleep like I do her sometimes.

I hope she doesn't fall in holes or forget to watch out for cars like I sometimes do when I'm thinking about her. I hope she's just fine like me.

One thing's really been making me lonelier than most, though.

I'd like to hear my name. Just once I'd like to walk up to somebody, tell them my name is Bird, and have them call me it.

Bird. Bird.

❀

"It's hard to get it off, isn't it?"

I look up and only see shadow. But I know who it is. Even though I haven't ever been close enough to hear him, I say, "Yeah."

"It gets all over the place," he says.

"Yeah," I say again.

"When I was little, I thought everybody in the world walked on red dirt roads, till we went to Colorado on the plane to see my cousins."

"No red dirt?"

"Nope. No red dirt."

The farm boy is still standing, so I feel like I should stand up too. He backs out of the shed and the sun pours down on my face.

He smiles.

Just like the pictures of him in the frames.

We both sit down under a big leafy bush, half burnt by the sun. We sit there looking off into the pond, not even talking anymore. It gets to be so quiet, I start to think I can hear his mom running water in her kitchen sink to wash dishes.

But that can't be.

It's just me wanting to hear the everyday stuff again. The noise a shower makes when it's just being turned off. Creaking steps and the way a key sounds going in a lock.

I move closer to the farm boy 'cause if we don't talk, maybe being close will help me feel the every-day stuff he's living.

So I just sit there, listening to the bees and frogs.

"Ethan," he says.

I move closer 'cause he smells like strawberry syrup.

"Bird," I say.

He smiles again, picks up a pebble, and throws it off into the field, then says,

"Bird. Bird."

And when he says my name, I see Cecil in his eyes.

5

ethan

SHE'S always hungry. I can tell. But she says she isn't. When I bring food out to her, she smiles, thanks me for it, and keeps on doing whatever it is she's doing.

We catch fireflies for an hour after I bring her out Mama's stew and corn bread. I don't know how she can smell the food and keep putting little bugs in jars.

But she does.

I leave her when I guess she won't eat with me there. Time I turn around to go home, I hear the foil crackling off the bowl of stew.

It's getting cooler at night, so yesterday I took Bird a blanket from the hall closet and a pillow off my sister's bed. She won't miss it. She must have about twenty of them. I don't know where she has room to sleep.

Bird.

That's her name. I like the way she says it.

Just Bird.

"You won't tell anybody I'm here, will you?"

"No."

It's raining, and Bird and me are sitting in the shed watching it fall hard on the ground.

"Thanks."

"No problem."

"You could get in trouble bringing me food and stuff."

"I won't."

"You could, though, 'cause I'm a runaway."

"It's okay. I don't think my parents would want you to starve and be cold just because you're a runaway."

"I guess so."

"I know so."

"You're okay, Ethan."

And after she says that, I am warm all over. Just so warm, I don't even feel the cool mist coming from the rain.

We run into the pond in our underwear.

I dive under first. There aren't too many more days it's going to be warm enough to jump in the pond.

Bird comes in after me, flapping her arms, eyes closed. Then she sinks up to her chin in water. She smiles, then sits in the water. I like being able to swim, because I never could before, and swimming with Bird makes it all good.

Bird, I figure, is just glad to be in water—feeling clean.

"This water is cold!"

"Yep. My sister says that there's prehistoric caves underneath this pond."

"You believe her, Ethan?"

"Kind of. Uh, well, maybe not a whole lot."

"But a little. You believe her a little bit."

"Yeah. A little."

Bird can swim better than anybody I've ever seen. She swims like one of those old catfish in the pond by the big gravel pit. She swims like she has gills, or maybe like she's a dolphin.

Like a dolphin, Bird swims.

I want to swim like her, but I'm still afraid. I touch my chest to check on the beating. I always do.

Then I start to swim after her.

"Yeah," she screams. "Come on, Ethan."

"I'm coming. Swim out to the middle."

We float for a long time and the water swirls around us. Like a whirlpool, only it's real gentle and doesn't pull us down like my sister says it will. And the sun is hot and helps us stay warm in the water.

Bird throws something green and slimy on me.

After I pull it off my face, I throw it back at her, but she dives underneath the water laughing like crazy. She comes up a few seconds later.

"Missed me!"

"Uh-uh. I got you before you went under."

"No, you missed me."

We stay out in the pond for a long time. When we start to feel tired, we float. And if you could see us from above, I guess you'd see two kids floating along in a circle (the whirlpool keeps us moving).

I get so tired, I almost go to sleep. But when my eyes open, Bird has swam over beside me. Ready to hold me up if I really go to sleep.

I smile at her wet face, wet braids.

When I walk into the yard, I see Uncle C.L.'s car. It's gray, old with a big dent in the back door. He's sitting on the front porch drinking a bottle of beer. I start running at him.

I don't even think about the look on his face when he sees me running across the yard. He meets me halfway up the steps, grabs me, then hugs me until I almost can't breathe.

Even though I'm too old to be hugging people, I do it anyway. After a while his face is wet. I can feel it on my neck.

"Got a new pump, huh, kid?"

"Yep."

Uncle C.L. keeps on holding me. "It's working okay?"

"Yeah."

"Well, that's all right then."

I leave him sitting on the porch. It's almost time to eat. I have to get food out for Bird before we sit down. Nobody will miss a couple of pork chops and vegetables. Mama made about five vegetables for Uncle C.L., so I grab a couple of them to make sure Bird eats before dark.

I walk into the kitchen, open the stove, and put two pork chops in a paper towel and scoop up black-eyed peas and cabbage greens in some foil.

I've only been taking food for Bird for a couple days. Today, I get caught.

Mama comes out of the store cupboard.

"What you doing with that food, Ethan? We're going to be eating in about ten minutes."

Mama is holding a jar of peach preserves in her hand and I'm trying to think of a lie, quick.

I say, "I'm hungry now."

Mama just shakes her head and tells me to put

the food back. "I'd like you to eat with the rest of us. It's your uncle C.L.'s first dinner here since you've been well."

And then Mama smiles, walks the couple of steps toward me in the warm and good-smelling kitchen, and runs her hand through my hair. She looks at the pork chops and peas, shakes her head again, and says, "Go on then."

When she turns her back, I run out the kitchen door, make sure she's not watching me (I catch her doing that a lot), then head off to find Bird.

But while I'm running, I think I see somebody out of the corner of my eye. When I turn around, the person's gone. So I try not to think about it. In a few minutes I'm at the shed at the end of the field.

I call her name soft at first. Then I look in the shed. Her backpack is gone. The blanket I got her is folded up. I know she hasn't just gone for a walk, because in the corner of the shed is a jar with pond weeds floating in it, and in the dirt beside it is written: *Bye*.

I leave the shed and walk the few feet to the

pond. It seems like a long time before I hear Mama's voice calling me home.

My uncle C.L. runs all the time when he comes to stay with us. Down the red dirt roads, across the dried-up cotton fields, and up the Atlanta Highway are his favorite places to run.

He says he started running when he was twelve to get out of his house and away from the beatings, so it's not hard to see that Uncle C.L. will always be running away from something. At least that's what Mama says. Her mom raised her, but C.L. got raised by their dad, who drank too much and had guns all over the house.

Uncle C.L. hates guns, anything loud, and can't stand meat.

When he stays with us, he goes to sleep at midnight, every time, wearing ear plugs and one of those sleep masks. Then, no matter what the weather is like, he gets up with the sun and runs.

I always wanted to run with him.

I used to crawl out of my warm bed to listen to the screen door swinging open and closed, the sound of tennis shoes swooshing down the steps and across the soft grass in the front yard.

He wears this shirt that says *runner*. Just *runner*. I wanted to run with him on those cool foggy mornings because it looked like he was running to something secret and would come back knowing something none of the rest of us did.

Daddy says it's a mania.

Yesterday I asked, "What's a mania?"

He spit out into the yard and leaned against the porch railings.

"It's something someone does that they can't help doing. They couldn't stop it if they wanted to. They'd need help stopping."

I said, "Then a mania is a bad thing."

Daddy blinked off into the sun and waved to Mr. Jakes as he blew past our house in the big green pickup.

"Uh-huh," he said.

I felt bad for Uncle C.L. All of a sudden his running wasn't the magic thing that it used to be to me. It wasn't that he was going out to find some kind of adventure, it was just that he couldn't help himself.

Then Daddy said something under his breath I guess he didn't mean for me to hear, but I did.

"Hell, if I'd been through what he'd been through, I guess I'd run too."

I started thinking about how when I could barely walk and my heart was almost gone, Uncle C.L. used to carry me on his back and take me anywhere I wanted to go.

I mean, man—we'd be gone . . .

Everywhere and nowhere.

He'd take me to the Red Bugle Club and we'd play the jukebox and drink Cokes all day long.

"Don't tell your mama we were here, okay?"

"I won't," I'd always say. I never did tell.

But then, after a few weeks or a couple of months, he'd leave.

He'd always leave when everybody was asleep.

We'd wake up in the morning and there'd be some kind of gift outside our door.

Uncle C.L. never said good-bye. I don't remember one time that we ever hugged him, said bye, and watched him walk out the door, get in his car, and drive away.

Mama says, "He doesn't have the stomach for it."

Like I don't have the stomach for butter beans, I guess.

HAVEN'T seen him in a long time. But here he is back again. I swear to God this dude must run a hundred miles a day. Only, where does he go? I only maybe see him for a month or two out of the year.

Maybe he's in the army and only comes to visit his family on leave. Maybe he works out at a gym most of the year and doesn't see the light of day the rest of the time. I don't know. But he's a good runner. Got his eyes on something looks like nobody else can see.

I know what that's like.

I open my bedroom window and climb out onto the tall hickory tree, then slide down only leaving about a third of my skin on the bark.

Forget about house arrest.

I'm about to go nuts staring at four walls, and I've memorized every poster, calendar, and even the number of basketballs on my side of the room.

Time to break.

Never been up and around at this time of the morning, but it's the only way I'm out of here. If I wait any longer, the old folks will be up and then it's just all of the same ole, same ole.

I didn't think people really got house arrest, but my parents talked to the judge about special circumstances—meaning me being a head case since Derek's been dead.

I'll bite. I don't mind being "troubled" if it keeps me out of juvy, which is where Googy is.

She called last night; rang the phone once, hung up, then rang again. The folks were in the front yard and didn't hear it, so this time we didn't need the code.

"What up, Jay?"

"Not much. You?"

I heard what sounded like a fight breaking out in the background. Googy screamed, "*Shut up!* I only got ten minutes on the phone and if you freaks mess with my time, I know something."

"Having fun, Goog?"

"Oh yeah. It's a party all around here."

I started feeling real bad. She's there and I'm here, and when you think about it, both of us stole the truck—even though she was driving it.

But in the end she got me out of it more than my parents did. She lied to the cop that she'd just picked me up and that I'd believed it was her uncle's truck. I thought I was gonna bust one listening to her lie. She was better at it than anybody I knew.

All she'd said to me when the siren got loud behind us and the cop stepped out of his cruiser was, "Don't say nothing. I'm on this."

I sat mute and just nodded my head when she talked.

Then she was gone for six months and I got house

arrest for three. I can only go to school. I didn't get one of those ankle bracelets that let 'em know when you're running, though.

"Your dad talking to you yet?" I said.

The phone got quiet. Finally Googy let out a breath.

"Nope. Hasn't come to see me yet either. I don't guess he will. I might get in the way of his life."

"How about your aunt?"

"Oh, yeah. Minna brought me cookies and dragged all one hundred of her bad kids here to visit. Some of the guards started looking at the ones under six like maybe they belong here too."

"Yeah, it's probably a future home for a couple of them. Especially that one who bites and throws rocks at cars all the time." I laughed.

"Uh-huh," Googy said.

We kept on talking; not really saying anything that's important, but everything that would make it feel like she was just at home and we'd see each other at school in the morning.

Now I know what people mean when they say

they're talking about nothing. Nothing makes you feel good sometimes.

I said bye to Googy when a voice warned us we only had one minute left.

Then, "Thanks, Googy. You didn't have to do what you did for me."

"Yes I did. Things have been sucking for you a lot lately, but not as long as *my* life has sucked, so I'm better at it. It's even kind of nice not to be at home with my dad. He wasn't ever there anyway . . ."

"Well, thanks—"

But the phone went dead.

I can't really keep up with the jogger. It's not like I'm really trying to. But it's something to do and I didn't even know I had this much energy.

He's probably about a quarter of a mile ahead of me. I keep him in view and try to run like him. Arms pumping, head straight up, and eyes looking ahead. But then he starts pulling away from me. It's like he's added a motor and gone into another gear.

I stop running because I can't get close now and

anyway it just feels good to be outside. My folks won't even let me out in the yard. I pretty much think the judge meant I had to stay on my parents' property, but the old folks are taking it to the limit.

I guess I breathe too much of the mist, because in a few minutes I'm coughing up a lung and almost have a heart attack when a girl is suddenly in front of me.

Figure she wasn't paying attention and just walked up on me.

Her eyes get big and she hollers.

I do too.

Then we both start laughing so hard that she drops her backpack and I have to hold my stomach, it hurts so much.

"Sorry," she says.

"No problem," I say. "Don't I know you? Are you somebody's cousin or something?"

She looks up the road, kicks a rock with her tennis shoe, and shakes her head.

"You go to my school?"

"No."

"Cool. I guess I don't know you."

She starts to walk away, then turns and says, "You and your friend covered me in dirt a couple of weeks ago with a truck. Then you got busted down the road."

I nod my head. "Yeah. That's you."

"Yep, that's me," she says, then starts walking again.

"Where you going?"

"That way." She points up the road.

"Want company?"

"Whatever," she says.

We must walk about a mile not saying anything to each other. She's wearing a hooded blue jacket and jeans. There's leaves on her back, and her hair needs to be combed. I start to wonder where she's come from.

I've lived in Acorn, Alabama, my whole life and only seen her twice.

By the time the sun has broken on through the mist, we're in town walking down the sidewalk past Oona's Cafe. The girl presses her face against the big window outside the restaurant.

"You hungry . . . ?"

"Bird. My name is Bird."

"You hungry, Bird?"

I know she's lying when she shakes her head.

"Well, I am. Come in here and sit with me awhile."

We're the first ones in Oona's this morning and Oona herself brings us the hard plastic menus, lays them on our table, and stares at me.

"Jay Hall, is that you?"

Oona's big blue hair is piled up high on her head. She probably weighs about seventy pounds—fifty of it hair. She wears cat eyeglasses and pops gum like the waitresses on TV do.

She knows everybody and everybody's business. So I'm busted. But she only shakes her head, looks at Bird, and says, "You want orange juice?"

And before she can answer, I say, "We both want the Early Bird."

Oona keeps shaking her head and trails on off to the kitchen.

Bird smiles.

I run faster than I've ever run in my whole life.

And not in a straight line . . .

I dodge behind buildings.

I jump behind trucks.

I hide for a minute behind a minivan because I could swear my mom is across the road buying something at the Saturday morning curb market by my school.

It isn't her, though.

Then I have to keep to the fields all the way home because cars are out now. Everybody gets up early on Saturday. Adults do at least. I think they're crazy. I'm only up and out because I'm not supposed to be.

By the time I get to the house and sneak through the back door and up the stairs, I hear somebody moving around.

I slide across the wooden hall floors and into my room, dive under the covers, and act like I'm sleeping in case the door opens in a few minutes.

Nobody in this house would believe I was awake this early in the morning for anything but the house being on fire.

"Jay?"

Mom pokes her head in my room. I don't answer.

"Jay?"

I fake a sleepy voice and drag my head from underneath the covers. "Hmmm?"

"What do you want for breakfast?"

"Not hungry."

I can feel her standing in the door not moving, wondering if she should come over, feel my forehead, then get out some medicine.

She stands there for about a minute before I hear the door close. Then I hear her talking to my pop and him saying, "He must not be sick, he hasn't been throwing up, has he?"

My pop's basic rule for sickness is if you haven't thrown up, you must be fine. Stripes on your face, 104 temperature, plus you've grown an extra arm? Go on to school, boy, you haven't thrown up.

Although, since Derek, I notice he stares at me longer before he asks if I've thrown up.

In a few seconds they go downstairs.

I sit up in bed and start counting the basketballs on the wallpaper again, but I only ever count the ones on my side of the room.

I leave Derek's side uncounted. I leave his side alone.

7
bird

I HAD a nightmare that I was the only person on a moving bus without a driver.

I kept passing my mom on the side of the road. The one thing I knew was that I had to get to the steering wheel. I knew if I got there, Cecil would show up and everything would be okay, even though sometimes he didn't show up in real life. He'd always forget me at dance class, and once when Mom was out of town, he forgot to come home and I was stuck on the porch until about ten o'clock at night.

I didn't tell Mom. She would have yelled.

Cecil just said, "Forgot about you, kid."

But I never see Cecil in the dream, just my mom standing on the side of the road.

I woke up thinking about the pictures. Cecil's family pictures. I knew Ethan before I met him. I remember Cecil taking the pictures out of my hand one afternoon when I found them in a duffel bag he kept in the hall closet.

"Stay out of my things. You don't know these people."

I wanted to say,

"But I know you, Cecil."

He'd been with me and Mom so long, I never thought about where he might have been before.

At the end of the dream, though, all I wanted the bus to do was fly.

Now my shoulders are sore from me jerking them in my sleep; trying to fly, I guess.

I thought I'd be in the shed forever. I believed all I had to do was wait and everything would work out. But when the time came, it didn't.

I watched him. I watched Ethan look for me in the shed, around it, and out over the field and pond. He was holding something in his hand. I guessed, by where the sun was in the sky, that it was my dinner.

I already miss Ethan. I guess I need more company than I thought. Maybe that's stupid 'cause it ain't like I'm going that far away, but that's the way it is.

"Where are you supposed to be, young miss?"

The old lady is all dressed in sky blue. I can't really see her face 'cause it's covered in some sort of net that's connected to a hat. She's wearing rubber gardening shoes and flowered work gloves.

When I sat down underneath these trees, I figured nobody could see me from the street. I'm pretty tired. But I guess most land belongs to somebody, so this bit must belong to her.

"Young miss?"

She's not going away. So I decide to run for it.

"Well, go on if you want," she calls. "I just thought you'd be a little company for me while I pull this nut grass."

Then she kneels down around a flowering bush

and starts pulling. Now I'm walking backward, looking at her. She's pulling grass and humming. Her voice makes me sleepy.

So I put my backpack up against a tree and sit back down cross-legged to watch her pull the nut grass, whatever that is.

There's one thing about the people in Alabama that I've never seen before in anybody else. They'll feed you if they think you're hungry, guess you're hungry, or if you aren't hungry but they are.

So here I am sitting on the porch of the big yellow house eating peach cobbler. A breeze blows and all the wind chimes hanging around the porch start singing. The sound is beautiful.

I stop eating and stand up to touch some of the chimes. My favorite one is of skinny long metal pipes almost as tall as me; you can probably hear them chime all over the neighborhood.

"Got those in a little shop in Japan."

Her face is nice. She has crinkling lines that turn up around her mouth like she must smile a lot. Her eyes sparkle too. I think she might just start laughing at something any minute.

I say, "I love them. I've never heard anything like them."

"Well. It's good to see or learn something new every day."

"I guess so," I say.

"I know so, young miss. Or maybe I should be calling you something different. Got another name besides *Miss*?"

"Bird. I like to be called Bird."

Then she sits down next to me in a painted white rocking chair, throws her head back, and laughs. Her laugh sounds like the wind chimes.

"I love your name, Bird. My name is Victoria Pritchard. When I was young, everyone called me Tori. My husband even married me because of my name."

"Really, he married you because he liked your name?"

She's smiling and looking at me like she's got a secret. "Umm-huh. But I guess there were other things about me that swayed him too. I could drive faster than him and knew more sports stats."

I scrape the last of the cobbler off the plate and empty the glass of lemonade.

"I don't know too much about sports except running."

Mrs. Pritchard waves away a fly.

"I love sports. I don't miss a Braves game if I can help it."

"Is that football?" I ask.

Mrs. Pritchard looks sorry for me, but laughs anyway.

"Baseball, Bird."

"Oh."

She rocks and says, "You don't have to know everything in the world. We aren't supposed to. It makes you boring in mixed company if you can't be interested and ask questions of other people."

"I guess so," I say again.

"So, where do you live, Bird?"

And it's out of my mouth so fast, I forget to lie. I forget Mrs. Pritchard isn't Ethan, or the boy who bought me breakfast this morning. She's a grown person. She could do something about me not being home.

"Ohio."

She shivers and says, "Ooh, they've got cold winters up there. Your family gonna stay here permanently?"

I shrug and hope she doesn't ask anything else about my family.

She says, "Well, I am tired."

I stand up. "I better get going."

"No need. It's just nap time. I take one in the late morning. Been doing that most of my life. You can stay here or come and get cleaned up in the restroom."

Then I know I'm not as invisible as I want to be and wonder just how bad I look.

Mrs. Pritchard waves me inside. I bring my plate and glass and walk into a cool, lemony-smelling house.

All the dark furniture shines. A ceiling fan blows the curtains by the front windows. Pictures of relatives are on the walls and all over tables.

I walk up the stairs with her.

"Bathroom, two doors down. Run yourself a bath, Miss Bird. Towels and everything are in there. I'll bring you a robe."

I'm between thanking Mrs. Pritchard and crying. I'm also thinking how she shouldn't be letting strange people in her house like she does. But I walk down the hall on shining wood floors and look into her bathroom.

She stands behind me, puts her hands on my shoulders, and says, "I'll make you a nice lunch after you've finished with your bath and taken a nap."

Then I do start to cry.

I used to hang out of trees when I was six, until I fell out of a maple and broke my arm. I was on a field trip with my class. My teacher, Miss Finch, kept apologizing to my mom at the hospital.

My mom kept saying, "Don't worry, don't worry about it. She's always falling."

And I was.

The first thing I remember was how my knee hurt when I fell on a sidewalk. Mom says I was almost three when that happened. I'd been holding crackers and wouldn't let my mom take them away from me even though they were all broken and bloody in my hands.

I can hold on for a long time to anything I want.

If I hadn't been holding on, I never would have seen Cecil yesterday. I knew he would come. I just knew it.

Cecil had stood in the back of the farmhouse stretching. I'd been waiting for Ethan to bring food. He always came on time, but yesterday he was so late, I moved closer to the house. That's when I saw Cecil.

I missed him so much all over again.

He hadn't said good-bye; he just left a box full of candles outside my bedroom door. He left Mom roses.

She threw them out, but I wouldn't burn my candles 'cause I didn't want them to end. Didn't want Cecil being with us to end.

But Cecil left Mom an address to send his mail. It was on top of the box of pictures. Mom says Cecil left it because his mind races and he forgets things. I decided to open the box—and there they were. The happy family.

The smiling family.

And he was right in the middle of them. Two boys, two girls, two grown people (maybe the kids' parents), and Cecil. They were all smiling in each and every picture in the box. What did these people know about Cecil that me and Mom didn't?

Were these the people he left us for?

So maybe if I got to know them or watched them . . .

That's when I decided I had to find him. I'd find out what made him happy in all those pictures, then me and Mom could do what the picture people did. It would be us all over again. Us being happy.

Cecil had lived with us for five years. And because I don't even remember my real father, he was all the dad I'd ever had.

My mom didn't believe in dating. Not before Cecil and not after. And I knew that between all the spending time with me and stuff to make me feel better about Cecil leaving, she would never let him come back on his own.

I had to find him and bring him back.

The waiting had been worth it. The hard nights and bug bites were worth it. The being lonely and hungry sometimes was even worth it. When I saw Cecil, it was all worth it.

But now I can't go to him 'cause what if it all doesn't matter. Maybe he'll say I could never be like his family. And now that they aren't just smiling people I never really met in pictures . . .

Go away, you're not my family is probably the worst thing he could say.

What if I ran crying into his arms and begged him to come back to Ohio with me and he just shook his head and sent me home without him?

So I'm running. Running scared.

Wish it had been as hard for him to leave me.

It's dark in the blue bedroom Mrs. Pritchard led me to after I took about a two-hour bath.

I had a tubful of bubbles and the whole bathroom smelled like lilacs. I stepped out of the tub onto a rug that was so soft, I wanted to curl up on it.

Then I wrapped up in a blue flowered robe that smelled the same as the bubbles. Mrs. Pritchard must love lilacs.

There was a knock on the bathroom door.

"Hi there, Miss Bird."

"Hi," I said.

"Well, I'm up from my nap. You look tired. Do you want to take one?"

Some part of me felt like I should say,

"No thanks."

Or,

"The bath was enough, and so was the cobbler and lemonade."

But I didn't. I let her show me to the bedroom next to the bathroom and don't remember anything after she said she had to garden and would wake me up in a while and give me lunch.

I wanted to say,

"You've been nice, Mrs. Pritchard, but I have to go."

Or,

"I don't want to take advantage, Mrs. Pritchard. You've been so nice to me."

But I didn't say any of that.

That's 'cause I didn't have anyplace to go. And after I sunk down into the bed and got comfortable, I didn't want to go anywhere.

Now the streetlight is on and it's not too dark in the bedroom. I walk across the carpet and open up the door.

Whatever's cooking makes my stomach jump, it smells so good.

I head for the food; down the stairs, across the living room, and into the biggest kitchen I've ever seen. They have these kinds of kitchens on television shows.

"Good evening, Miss Bird."

"How you doing, Mrs. Pritchard?"

"Just fine. You hungry?"

"Yes please."

I sit down at the round wooden table. It's huge, but the kitchen is ten times bigger. The counters gleam white and the walls are green. I move a pair of chicken salt and pepper shakers around like they're chasing each other.

Mrs. Pritchard puts a big plate of pot roast, potatoes, glazed carrots, collard greens, and corn bread in front of me. She sits down in the chair across the table from me, smiles, and says,

"We don't have to talk. You just eat till you're full. There's more on the stove."

I do what she says and have never had better food in my whole life. This food is even better than when Cecil made homemade French fries and let me eat as many as I wanted with ketchup, which was a dream of mine. (I only got junk food after Cecil left 'cause Mom didn't have the energy to cook anymore.)

I finish eating and shake my head when Mrs. Pritchard offers me a third plate of food.

"I'm full now, thanks. It was some of the best food I ever had."

"Why, thank you, Miss Bird."

I snuggle into the robe, then get up to help with the dishes. I dry everything that Mrs. Pritchard hands me, standing at the sink. She's in a flowered housedress now and humming the same song as before.

I start yawning.

"Where's your family, Miss Bird?"

"Ohio," I say.

"Are they there now?"

I don't say anything.

"Are they so far away that you'll need a place to stay while you're visiting?"

I dry a glass for about two minutes. After a while I nod.

Mrs. Pritchard says, "Well, Miss Bird, I got room and you need a room. Why don't we talk about your people tomorrow and let you get some more sleep tonight. Deal?"

I nod my head.

Mrs. Pritchard starts humming again, then a little while later she talks about how her sister Claire couldn't grow weeds in an overgrown field.

I laugh at her Claire stories while moths flutter outside the kitchen window.

8
ethan

I SLEPT on top of our roof last night. You wouldn't believe what you can see from the top of a house. I think I might have seen all of Macon County.

Nobody knows I was up there, except maybe Uncle C.L., who looks at me kind of funny this morning. It was hard getting up there. I had to grab hold of the built-in emergency ladder. You're not supposed to go up it, so it took a little time.

I had to stretch, while my feet were on the third top rung, and grab hold of the gutter without tearing it off the roof and killing myself in a three-story fall.

I made it, though. And I made it without waking up the whole house.

At first I wanted to see if I could spot Bird from the roof. She didn't leave a note, just *Bye* in the dirt. I got worried that somebody found her out here, but the way the blanket was folded and then the jar . . .

I figure it was just time for her to go and she didn't want to say good-bye.

I still want to know where she is.

I miss her.

I miss her and can't tell anybody about it. Not even Uncle C.L., though I think he might understand all about not telling on a runaway who's been living in our shed waiting for someone. She wouldn't tell me who it is, but the person must be special.

Anyway, I've been getting these feelings lately. I don't know what to call 'em, but they make me want to do things I never did before. I think it's my heart, or at least, I think it's the heart that used to belong to somebody else.

I want to eat things that I never wanted before,

like eggs, peanut butter, and anything green.

Sometimes I think somebody is in my room with me. Then I'm thinking it's the boy who gave me his heart. I don't see him or anything. That would be too scary and I don't want to believe in ghosts.

I just feel like there's somebody . . .

And that's what I felt like when I climbed up on the roof last night. I was always afraid of heights, always.

Since nobody ever made me do anything I was afraid of because I was so sick, I figured I'd be afraid forever. But I'm not anymore, and last night I wanted to climb.

I wanted to see everything out there in the starlight. I wanted to see the lights down the street on the McCullens' farm. I wanted to see the pump lights from Harold's Gas and Tires. I even wanted to see the parking lights go out as people rolled out of their cars at the Red Bugle.

And I wanted to see Bird. But she doesn't glow in the dark. At least I don't think she does.

I'd tied a blanket around my waist before I

climbed out the hall window because I was going to sleep all night on the roof. There's a flat part of the roof by the chimney that's good for sleeping. I wanted to feel what it was like to camp out. I used to listen to kids in Sunday school talk about it.

It was a dream: campfires, food cooked outside, and ghost stories while it got darker in the woods, and it was something I was never gonna be allowed to do while I was sick. But now I don't need the woods or a campfire to feel what I missed.

All I needed last night was my blanket underneath me and the one million stars above me.

It would have been nice having Bird there too. She could have told me stuff about the Greyhound bus and what it was like to be so far away from home. We could have talked all night long and laughed.

Or we could have just been there on the roof not saying anything because we were together.

Mama is standing at the sink and Daddy's pouring pancake batter on the griddle.

"Damn!"

"You know, Curtis, not everybody gets attacked by stoves like you do," Mama says.

Daddy shrugs.

"And keep the damning down, it's Sunday."

"Better to mess up on Sunday. I can think about trying to do better while I'm sleeping during the sermon."

Mama hits him with a towel. "Heathen."

Daddy looks at me and winks.

Uncle C.L. pulls up the chair beside me and puts my napkin over my head.

"What up, dog?"

He looks up toward the ceiling and then starts to drink the coffee Mama put in front of him.

"Nothing," I say.

"Nothing, huh?"

"Yep."

"Hmmm. I swear nothing must be going on with millions of thirteen-year-old boys. At least if you ask them, that's what they'll say."

Mama and Daddy start to load up the table.

Pancakes, sausage and bacon, toast, home fries and grits, eggs, and fruit salad along with juice, coffee, and cinnamon rolls almost spill over the sides. I start to wonder where Nonie is going to put her plate.

She wanders down a few minutes later in an old T-shirt and shorts, yawning. "We feeding a football team or what this morning?" she says.

She moves some food aside and grabs for the coffee. "This is what I need."

I look around the table, but what I really want isn't there. Mama looks at me, gets up, opens the cabinet, and brings me peanut butter.

Daddy turns his nose up when I dip my bacon in it.

Nonie says, "Ma, you gonna let that kid eat all that fat? Gross. Stop him."

Mama ignores her and keeps eating her breakfast, while Uncle C.L. and Daddy talk about the new dog track.

Nonie starts kicking her chair leg.

"Racing dogs is immoral and cruel. What's wrong with those people? Why don't they tie a number on the owners and send *them* around the track chasing a mechanical steak?"

Uncle C.L. cracks up and chokes on his coffee.

Daddy shakes his head and smiles.

Mama looks at Nonie, then passes her a cinnamon roll because she stopped eating meat a few days ago.

"Tell it like it is, baby."

Then they talk about the dogs and everything in between. Sometimes Uncle C.L. looks over at me and smiles. I just dip things in peanut butter and think about how if Bird doesn't show up in a couple of days, I should go looking for her.

Then I start thinking about how I can now. I can go looking for her in the woods and fields. I can walk, even run, up the road to find her and I won't get out of breath or start to feel sick.

I could go up the road and maybe if I don't find her, I'll run into some of the kids in my class. Since it's the first year I get to go to school, they're all new to me. I could hang out with them. Go to Ponchos and have root beer floats or whatever some of them do when they're just hanging.

I was never able to just hang like my brother, David, and my sisters, Nonie and Anna Mae. Anna Mae is married and lives in Florida. But I bet she always had a good time because when I think of her, I see her laughing.

Mama and Uncle C.L. are clearing the table. Nonie is fighting with Daddy about people chopping pulp wood, and I listen to all of them as I find a paper plate, load it up with food, and put it in the cabinet full of spices.

The food is for Bird even though I don't think she'll be back for it today, or use the tub or take a nap on the couch. But that's all right. She might.

I make sure the strawberry syrup is on the counter and that there aren't any clothes in the washer or dryer in case she wants to use them.

Then I wish.

Wish for Bird to come back.

Wish that Uncle C.L. will stay a long time.

Wish that if I have to go looking for Bird, I find her.

I feel sleepy next to Nonie as the car leaves the

driveway on the way to church. Uncle C.L. runs beside the car in his "runner" T-shirt, and by the time we get to the turnoff and leave him in a big cloud of red dirt, I'm asleep.

9
jay

RAY Walter and Ricky play with the Rock 'Em Sock 'Em Robots Derek and me got for Christmas two years ago. They get into it so much, the walls start shaking.

"Shut up. My mom's gonna hear you," I say.

Ray Walter yells, "C'mon, c'mon! Go, go—ahhh . . ."

Ricky jumps up and down like he's won the heavyweight championship.

"I'm the champ. Smack down!"

"Yeah, yeah, you're the champ. Sit down, man," I say, grinning.

They aren't supposed to be up here. But here they are. And here I am knowing my room-prison time is supposed to be spent alone. If I get busted with the Louds here, all hell will break loose. But the guys are funny and I miss Googy.

Ricky must read my mind.

"So how's your girl, man?"

"Okay. She's doing what she can to stay out of trouble."

Ray Walter puts on a pig mask that's lying on the floor.

"Remember when she put live chickens in all the bathrooms at school? Man, I thought I was gonna fall out over that one."

I start laughing.

"And when the principal figured out she'd done it and told her to get the chickens out—"

"She left school and came back with flour, cooking oil, and salt. Then told Mr. Julien she hoped they'd left the cafeteria open." Ricky laughs.

"Yeah," I say. "Googy is too much."

"You must miss her, huh?" Ricky says. "I mean, I

don't think I ever saw one of you without the other."

I shrug about missing her. It's not that I don't. And it's not that I mind him asking. It's just private. I don't want to talk about how I miss her or how I get ready to tell a funny story and she isn't there.

I miss her.

"When you getting out of here, Jay?" Ray asks.

"I got three months under house arrest."

"It should go by fast." Ricky says, then twists a pair of dog puppets around his arm till I guess he sees me looking at him like he's whacked.

"What?" Ricky says.

"Nothing."

"What, Jay?"

Ray Walter looks around the room and must finally notice something.

He crawls across the floor to Ricky and whispers, "This is Derek's stuff, man. Put it down."

"Sorry, Jay."

"No problem. I mean, it's just there. We haven't put stuff away. I feel better with it there, I guess."

"Yeah, I get that," Ricky says.

"Wanna go out to the pond?" I say.

"Yeah, let's break out of here. You gonna get caught, Jay?" Ricky looks out of the bedroom door like he's a spy or something.

"I do it all the time. My folks are leaving in a minute to go to one of those grief meetings. They don't even think about me when they get back home."

Since Ray Walter and Rikki sneaked in, they have to hide in the closet when my mom knocks on the door to say good-bye.

She has her dark glasses on already.

"There's soup and salad downstairs, Jay."

"Cool," I say.

"Be good, okay?"

"What else am I going to be?"

"All right then."

But she doesn't leave; she walks in and hugs me. She smells like honey and roses. She spends a lot of time with her roses now. She gardens more than she does anything. Her beaded braids are covered with a scarf. It makes her look like one of those old-time movie stars.

Looks like she should be saying, "No pictures, no pictures."

"I'll be fine, Mom."

"I know you will."

But something about the way she holds me tells me she doesn't really believe it. Finally she goes, and Ricky and Ray Walter fall out of the closet.

"Geez," Ray Walter whines. "There's no room in that closet."

"Yeah," Ricky says, pulling a sweatshirt off his back and kicking a tennis racket and ball into the mess.

"It's a closet, man. There's not supposed to be room for two people *and* the closet mess," I say, looking out my bedroom window to make sure my mom and pop are gone before we leave.

Ricky and Ray Walter chase after me like a pair of clumsy puppies down the stairs and into the kitchen.

What I don't eat, they do, which is a whole lot of food.

Then we head out into the woods and a long walk

to the pond past the field I used to play in every day when I was little. Can't believe I used to go there every day. It must be miles to the pond from my house.

I thought places were supposed to shrink.

It's okay hangin' with Ray Walter and Ricky even though all they want to do is tell dumb stories and throw things in the water.

I don't have to think about much when I'm with them. Nothing is serious. God, nothing will ever be serious with them. Guess I can only take so much of being by myself.

"Watch this, Ray."

Ricky throws half a tree into the pond and splashes a ton of water out. Ray Walter laughs like it's the funniest thing he's ever seen. I even laugh a little.

I'm soaking wet by now, but I don't worry about it.

Ray Walter looks like a drowned rat, but Ricky is still dry and laughing at us.

Ray Walter looks at me, then at Ricky, and I know what we have to do.

"Get him!" we holler at the same time, running around the bank of the pond. We finally catch up to Ricky by an old willow, and grab him by the legs and arms.

Soon we're all in the pond and I'm having the best time. And for about one whole minute I laugh till my jaw hurts. When it's all done and I'm spitting pond water out of my mouth, I don't even feel bad about being happy.

After dunking everybody and them dunking me, I start swimming back to land, and that's when I see Bird.

"Hey." She waves to me, then puts her backpack down on the ground.

Ray Walter and Ricky swim over to me.

"Who's that?" they say together.

I look over at Bird and remember that day at Oona's and what we'd talked about afterward.

"She's my cousin," I say, swimming to shore.

Ricky and Ray Walter aren't interested anymore. Hell, everybody has cousins. That's never anything big in Acorn. They go back to splashing around the water and ignoring us.

"How you doing?" I say.

"Fine."

"Want to go for a swim?"

Bird watches Ray Walter and Ricky for a minute and starts laughing.

"It looks fun, but no. I don't want to walk around in wet clothes all day."

I never thought about her not having a bathing suit or anything. Me and the boys are in our underwear. I guess it's different for girls.

While Bird watches all the splashing in the pond, I put my pants and shirt on.

She says, "I don't know why they call this place a pond. It's more like a lake, don't you think?"

I look across it.

It is kinda big enough to be a lake. I just never thought about it because everybody in Acorn calls it a pond.

"Guess so," I say, then sit down underneath the tree.

We don't talk.

I don't tell her how I thought about her the other day when it was raining. I wondered if she had found a place to go.

She looks better today than she did on Saturday.

Her hair is combed and she looks clean and not hungry, but I don't think I should mention it. Maybe that's being nosy. So I say,

"I broke out again."

She laughs. "You're a serious outlaw, man."

"Yep. One of those house arrest outlaws."

"What'll happen if they catch you?"

"Can't think about that, or I'd never have any fun."

Bird smiles.

"My brother sure did like to swim."

As I'm saying it, I don't believe it's coming out of my mouth. I even look around for somebody who sounds like me to be standing off to the side.

Bird pitches a rock into the water.

"Why isn't he here with you? Will he tell?"

"He's dead," I say.

And it's the first time I've said those words.

It's the first time those words fell out of my mouth.

Those two words feel like cold metal on my tongue. What they must have felt like in my stomach, I don't know.

I look at Bird. She doesn't say anything when she reaches over and holds my hand.

I want to ask her what she's doing here, so the metal will leave my mouth. But I can't talk. And I'm wondering how some runaway girl I've only met once before got me to say the words.

It might be a minute or it might be five hours later when Bird twists around and starts staring across the field like she's waiting for somebody to show up.

But a few seconds later she turns back to the pond and says,

"They really should call this place a lake."

10
bird

ETHAN holds his chest when he talks and Jay talks like his heart is in his hands.

Even in this little town I don't think they know each other. Jay says his family has only lived here a few years. Ethan has been here his whole life and is younger than Jay.

I don't mention one to the other, but something tells me I'm right about them anyway.

I miss my mom.

I even miss the people here that I can see every day if I want. 'Cause they aren't mine. All these people going in and out of their houses in this place I'm gonna leave anytime—they don't belong to me.

I'm borrowing them until I get what I came for.

Hope it's not wrong to borrow them. It doesn't mean I don't like them or care about them. I'm only passing through and borrowing.

A few years ago I got lost at a carnival. One minute Mom and Cecil were there, the next, they were gone. I got scared after about twenty minutes and almost started crying.

Then I saw Cecil. At least I thought I did. I ran up to the back of a man who looked just like him and grabbed his hand. The man said,

"I don't believe I belong to you, little girl."

And then I really did start to cry.

Later, when I was home again and safe, just thinking about the man saying he didn't belong to me made me sadder than I ever thought I could be.

I've been watching Cecil when he runs past Line

Creek. I can't keep up with him, so I had to guess where he'd go. Back home he'd always run down by the river. He said the running water relaxed him.

It's been five days of watching him run through the tall grass and some of the marshy places. He still wears his "runner" T-shirt.

I have to leave Mrs. Pritchard's house early in the morning to watch him. Then I stay gone the rest of the day so me and Mrs. Pritchard can make believe I'm going to school and she doesn't have to feel guilty about not turning me in.

We're good at make-believe.

Maybe Mrs. Pritchard just wants the company. I know I need her company. I'm looking for somebody and too afraid to tell 'em I'm here, and she's just lonely and looking for company.

I remember something that made my heart ache the other day. Ethan leaned against Cecil in the backyard of the farmhouse. I watched from the field and my heart was beating so much, I thought it was going to jump right out of my chest. It hurt.

I wanted to be where Ethan was. Cecil talks quiet

and sometimes you have to lean in to hear him. I never told Ethan I knew Cecil, but I told him not to tell anybody about me.

Would he have been as friendly if he knew I wanted to take his uncle C.L. back with me when all he could talk about was how he wanted him to stay?

So I keep watching and know the time is coming to take Cecil back. Back to everything he knew and left in Ohio. Back to my mom and back to me.

11
ethan

I WATCH Bird heading toward me. My heart beats faster. I'm still getting used to it beating so strong.

"Bird, I didn't know when you'd come back."

She sits down in the tall grass and pulls blades up, then throws them at me.

"You hungry?" I say.

"No, Ethan. I'm okay," she says.

"You look like you're fine."

"I am fine, Ethan."

Bird unzips her backpack and pulls out a plastic bag of crackers. She holds the bag out and even though I'm not hungry, I take a couple crackers and eat them.

"It feels good to be able to give somebody something to eat," she says.

"Yeah," I say.

Bird falls back and starts looking up at the sky.

"I think the sky is bluer in Alabama, Ethan."

"Don't really know if it is. I never looked up at any other state's sky. You think this sky is better than the others?"

"It's better than the sky I can barely see back in Cleveland."

"What's that sky like?" I say.

Bird closes her eyes, then I lie down and look up at the sky like she was. I hope she comes back and stays in the shed. I don't know how to ask her to come back, though.

So I just look up at the birds and the clouds moving in and out of the sun.

"You been hangin' out, Ethan, trying to make friends?"

I lie. "Yeah."

Bird stretches. "What was it like not to have to go to school all that time?"

"I had school. I just had it at home, the hospital . . . My mama taught me and sometimes there was a tutor from the county board."

"You really must have been sick, huh?"

"I guess so. I mean, I know so," I say.

"He never said nothing to us about it . . ."

"Who never said anything about what?"

Bird sits up, shades her eyes from the sun.

"Ethan, you think somebody can love a person if they don't tell that person things about themselves?"

"Don't know, Bird. I barely know enough people. I know doctors and nurses. I've met a lot of sick kids who were at the hospital."

"Did you get to be friends?"

I keep watching the birds.

"Ethan?"

"Sometimes it's not a good idea to make friends with people who might not be there the next day. It's just some more people you have to miss. Sick kids . . . Some of them went home in a few days . . ."

"Oh," she says.

I ask again, "Who didn't tell you about what?"

"Forget about it." She leans over and touches my chest. I almost jump out of my skin.

"It doesn't still hurt, does it?" she asks.

"No, it's perfect now."

"Good. Now that you have a perfect heart, what do you think you'll do with it?"

I start laughing. Bird looks at me like she doesn't understand.

"Really. What you gonna do with it? It's a gift, you know. Somebody up and gave you a gift. People like to see people using their gifts."

"I can't wear my heart like a new T-shirt or a baseball cap, Bird."

"Uh-huh," she says.

"I can't. That's . . . I don't know. What do you mean?"

The sun disappears behind the fluffiest white clouds I've ever seen. I watch Bird and want to understand what she's talking about, and notice she's wearing an afro for the first time.

"Where's the rest of your hair, Bird?"

"In a trash can in town. I don't miss it. This kind of hair is easy to take care of."

"I like it," I say.

"Well, that's okay then." She laughs.

"I have to go now. My uncle C.L. and me are gonna do some stuff. I don't guess you want to meet him. Do you?"

Bird sits up and looks toward our house. Then she stands, grabs her backpack, takes some more crackers out of it, and says,

"You go on. I got to get back."

"Where you going back to Bird? You haven't told me where you're at."

Then she looks at me, mad.

"You need to get some friends, Ethan. I don't live in this place, you know. You ain't my family or anything. When are you gonna . . . ?"

"Gonna what?"

Here I'm standing, not knowing why all of a sudden Bird isn't Bird anymore. Why is she so mad? I can't even start thinking about what I did to her.

Then she heads off toward the pond. I want to run after her. I really do. I want to tell her she's the only one outside family and hospital people that I ever had to talk to.

She keeps walking.

Then she turns around. "I love you, Ce—Ethan."

Then she's running.

My arms are lighter when I walk back to the house.

Mama and Uncle C.L. are laughing on the back porch and the radio is playing. I stand between them, then sit down.

Uncle C.L. palms my head.

"What up, nephew?"

"Nothing," I say. "Nothing at all."

12

jay

"YOU look good, Googy."

"How did you get here?" she says. "How did you get in?"

She's wearing what the rest of the kids wear here. A light blue shirt and blue jeans with white tennis shoes. No jewelry, nothing in her hair.

But she's still got attitude and only nods her head a fraction when somebody calls out her name from across the room and waves.

She's smiling so hard at me, though, she almost

blows 'tude. Nobody here probably ever has seen her smile.

Her smile lights up the place.

"Are you deaf, Jay? How did you get in here?"

"See that woman?" I point across the room to a skinny woman with three kids, visiting a girl who's holding one of her little sisters. "I stood out by the gates and asked people if I could go in with them. She said it was okay with her, I could be her son that was on the list but had to work today. They don't hassle minors who visit with parents."

"I was buggin'. I really did need a visitor. Even though Minna comes . . . Ooh, those kids. She can't afford a sitter, but I ain't about to complain."

"I'm here," I say.

"It's good seeing you, except for the fact you gonna probably be in the boys' section in about a minute. How did you get out?"

"Magic," I say.

Googy laughs and I'm so glad to see her again, I almost forget we're in an ugly green room with plastic chairs and posters tacked up everywhere about drugs and AIDS.

"We use this place for assemblies. But they usually don't last long 'cause a knife fight or something always breaks out," Googy says.

"Damn."

"I'm used to it," she says.

"I guess so, huh?" I look around. "These kids could be anybody at our school. I guess they are anybody at some school."

"Yep. Did you write your letter yet?"

"I forgot all about that," I say. But I'm lying.

We talk about everything and nothing for forty-five minutes. That's all the time we have. Googy says that you only get thirty minutes at the county jail.

When it's time for me to go, I hug her and pull the envelope out of my pocket. She opens it and laughs. It's a picture of us at the zoo the time an anteater just about freaked her out.

In the picture she's screaming and holding on to me and I'm laughing and holding on to her to stay up.

She walks me to the door and presses a buzzer so the guard can let me out.

When I'm almost through the door she says,

"I dreamed about you and Derek last night. It was real weird. A bird had let you both out of a locked room. How you think something like that can happen, huh?"

Then she waves, leaning against the ugly green table. "Only in dreams, huh, bro? Only in dreams."

It's not until after I hitch a ride back into town and am sneaking back into the house that I think about the bird and dreams.

I've seen that woman about six or seven times do what she's doing now.

It's the same, every time.

She drives up, parks on the side of the road, then gets out and opens up the trunk. She takes out a bag of dirt, a bucket, and some garden tools. Then puts everything in the front yard.

Then he gets out, opens the back door, and lifts out a rosebush. He takes it over to her and they go to work and never say a word to each other. They know what to do.

Nobody ever comes out of our house to thank them, complain, or even tell them to go away. It's like the most normal thing in the world for these people we don't know to show up every so often and plant roses in our yard.

I never watch her.

I just watch him—the boy—and never can tell how I feel about seeing him. And then I think how the next time they come here, I'm going to run outside and tell them not to ever come into our damn yard again.

But I don't.

It's like I'm stuck to the floor when they're diggin' in the dirt trying to thank us some way.

I don't go to church anymore because I don't want to be that close to them. Mom and Pop still go and never say a word to them or about them.

Roses for a heart.

❀

Mrs. Pritchard,

I used to fight with my little brother, a lot. Maybe that's not the way to start out a forgiveness and I'm sorry letter, but looks like this is how it has to be.

Anyway, we fought so much, one of us was always getting in trouble for it.

I guess it's the kind of thing brothers do to each other. Take video games, lose clothes, borrow stuff and don't ask.

But once I did something to my little brother I couldn't ever take back.

I didn't know I would do it, it just happened on his last birthday.

During his party (he had about ten friends over for pizza) he started opening his gifts. He got a game that I'd wanted for a long time. So when I said, "Man, I can't believe you got that before me," he says, "And I'm gonna invite everybody up to my room to play it except you."

I could have let it go.

It was his birthday party.

But I said it. I said the one thing. I said, "I hope nobody sits on your bed because they'll smell like pee after it's all over."

A couple of his friends laughed, but most of them just looked down and probably started thinking maybe this was the reason he never ever came to sleep-overs.

Derek ran out of the house.

The party was over.

Mom said I took something from Derek that day that I might never get back. I told her I didn't take anything from him. She just walked away and said figure it out.

I was still trying to figure it out until just a little while ago. One, because I have to see the judge next week and let him read this letter. Two and most important, I know what I took from my brother and you.

Trust. That must be it because now I remember how Derek would look at me when he'd bring his friends around (he didn't bring them over too much after the party).

And now I'm remembering the lemonade and how we

used to talk and how I used to laugh and say anything I felt around you.

I'm sorry if I took from you what I took from my brother.

I didn't make it right with him.

Can I make it right with you?

I'm sorry.

Jay

16
bird

MRS. PRITCHARD'S waxing the old truck when I walk up the sidewalk and into the drive.

"I like your truck, Mrs. Pritchard."

"She's a nice ole thing, isn't she, Miss Bird?"

"Yeah, she is."

I go over and look at my reflection in the driver's side door. It's like glass.

The truck looks old. Real old.

"Do you drive her?"

"Not anymore. But my son comes by ever so often and starts her up. This old truck's been here a long time. It's seen about twelve presidents come and go and it's still running."

"So you used to drive it."

Mrs. Pritchard keeps on waxing the truck in a lilac-covered housedress. She's wearing a straw sun hat and old mules. She smiles at me but doesn't answer.

"Can I help?" I ask.

"Please do."

I take one of the big white towels she's using and start dipping it in wax and swirling the wax on, then buffing it off. It's relaxing; I don't think about Cecil while I'm doing it.

Funny, back home this would have felt like work to me. I would've whined about Mom making me do hard jobs. Now I'll do anything to help Mrs. Pritchard.

Sleeping in a warm bed and eating good hot food and not fighting bugs is worth about a million dollars. I couldn't ever pay her back.

We work while the leaves move soft in the big trees over the driveway. We work until my arms feel like they're going to fall off. When the truck's finally shining like a store window, I stand back with Mrs. Pritchard and look at it.

She puts her arm around me.

"Where's your family right now, Miss Bird?"

I turn and look at her.

"Some of it's here and some of it's up there in Ohio."

"I see," she says.

"Most of the time I don't see it. I don't get it at all."

Mrs. Pritchard walks me away from the truck, across the lawn, and up the steps of the porch.

"Is home that bad, Miss Bird?"

I can't answer that 'cause if I say it is, she'll think somebody's hurting me. She won't think being left is the same thing.

I used to hear stories about why people ran away. Mine wasn't scary like theirs.

No broken bones or smashed faces ever happened to me that I didn't give to myself.

I had food and clothes. I had my mom. I had Cecil.

No broken bones for me, so home must not have been bad.

The chimes start swinging in the wind.

No broken bones.

I don't want to get up this morning. I curl up tighter underneath the blankets Mrs. Pritchard has made sure are at the foot of my bed every night, "in case of frost."

I want to have a hot breakfast and go wandering around Acorn, which I can only do on the weekends. People stare at you around here if it's a school day and you aren't there. In Cleveland, nobody would even notice.

But I get up.

I put on my sweatpants, T-shirt, and hooded jacket. I leave my backpack, open my door, and head down the stairs and to the back door in the kitchen to get my shoes.

Mrs. Pritchard is already up at five in the morning, sipping coffee.

"So there you are."

"Uh-huh," I mumble 'cause she almost scared me to death.

"You need breakfast, Miss Bird?"

I get my shoes and bring them back to the table to put them on.

"No thank you," I say.

"Orange juice?"

"That would be good 'cause I'm goin' on a run this morning."

She goes to the fridge and takes out the orange juice, then pours it in a glass that's sitting at my place already. Funny how I've already got a place here.

I drink every drop, tie my shoes, and get up to go.

"I hope you catch what you're running at, Miss Bird. I sure do hope you catch it."

"Hope I do too," I say, and walk on out the door into the cool misty Alabama morning. And since I'm still up before most people, the whole world smells different than it will in even an hour.

14
ethan

HE left a minute ago. I heard the door open and his feet run down the steps and swish across the grass.

This morning I want to get up and run with Uncle C.L. I want to jog with him and only hear our breathing down the red dirt paths, past the dark houses and fields, up the Atlanta Highway and down Line Creek.

But I don't.

I pull the blankets over my head, sink down further into bed, and fall back to sleep. I don't know how long I'm asleep, though, before I wake up and hear Bird calling me.

It's still dark enough that I can't see without a light when I get out of bed and go over to my window.

Where's she at?

She's calling my name somewhere, but not anyplace I can see. I go downstairs to the living room, wrap up in one of the blankets from the chest, and fall back to sleep, dreaming of playing football with the whole school cheering.

At the end of the dream I'm surrounded by people and feeling real warm. Warm like you feel when you get a gift you're not expecting.

Then I start thinking maybe that's what Bird meant when I saw her a few days ago. I want to go back to the dream, but I hear somebody moving around upstairs and I know it's really time to get up.

I like the school bus because I'm a watcher.

There's the kids like me. We usually sit in the middle of the bus so we can check everybody out.

Then there's the real smart ones who sit anywhere and block everybody out while they're reading or doing more work. The scared kids try to sit close to the bus driver and the hoods sit where they want and do whatever they want.

Everybody else just sits with their friends or wherever there's a seat.

Today one of the watchers sits down next to me.

"Hey," he says.

"What's up?" I say.

He drops his backpack, skateboard, and a big glass jar of something blue and fuzzy on the seat between us.

"It's fungus," he says.

"Oh yeah? Where can *I* get some of that?" I say, pushing it away from me.

"Paco," he says.

"Ethan," I say.

"You new or what?" he asks.

"What," I say.

He laughs and starts telling me about skateboards.

Somebody screams for somebody else to give

them back their lunch and the bus driver screams that if he hears any more noise, he's gonna get everybody off the damned bus.

By the time the bus pulls into school, I've forgotten about the dream.

Two things I remember.

Once, when I could barely breathe and was in a wheelchair, my sister Nonie and some of her friends dressed up like characters from my favorite comic books.

Magneto, Iron Man, Silver Surfer, and Hawkeye ran around the hospital most of the afternoon and read kids books, played games, and sang off-key. I remember that I knew I was going to die and I was so tired of fighting that I wanted to let go as I watched the superheroes and villains running through the rooms.

The next thing was listening to some nurses talking in the hall about a boy who had passed out on the school bus and was brain-dead. But it looked like the parents were about to be talked into giving his heart away, to me.

I can remember like it was five minutes ago how I felt each time.

Tired and just wanting to sleep.

Then tired and wanting to get up, run around, and scream. So when I start to think about it, I just want to run. Just like my uncle C.L.—except one day I'd want to stop and be in one place.

I don't think Uncle C.L. ever will.

He's always gonna keep running.

So I'm gonna just be around till he goes away again, because there's nothing to do to stop him. Mama says at least he always comes back home.

That's okay too.

15

jay

SOMETHING made me do this and I don't know what it is. But I'm doing it. I'm going to take the letter to Mrs. Pritchard myself.

That means I have to break out one more time.

I've broken out so much, it's almost a laugh, but I'm starting to feel bad, thinking about how Googy isn't going anywhere.

I could ask to go, but it wouldn't do any good because to my mom, the law is the law. That's it. I guess that's why I made myself think it was okay.

It's still dark out when I sneak down the stairs

one last time. And after I open the front door and the cool wet hits me in the face, I want to go back to bed and just be happy I got off so easy.

But I don't.

I start jogging into town, keeping to the middle of the road where I know it's smooth and I'm not liable to break an ankle.

Early morning is different than any other time I know. It's right when the night people have been asleep for about two hours, and two hours before the day people get into it.

But even better this morning is the runner. At first I don't recognize the sound, then I know it's tennis shoes pounding the ground. I must be close to him. Real close.

I know it's him now—arms pumping, head straight up. It'll be no time till I get to town now, following the runner. And in no time I'm running under streetlights and dodging parked cars.

By the time I turn down Overlook Steet, the runner is gone and I'm at the big yellow house that doesn't have any color right now in the dark.

But I'm feeling dumb now.

What am I gonna do? Wake an old lady up before six in the morning because I feel bad about everything I did and about Googy?

That's when I decide to turn around and go home.

I'll leave the letter in the box. I've had enough of this getting up, chasing runners, and hangin' with runaway girls and feeling so bad about old ladies.

But the next thing I know, I'm on the big porch sitting in an old rocking chair crying like a baby. And all I can think is how glad I am it's so dark and how bad I miss my brother.

By the time I notice someone's standing in the door, the porch light's on and it's too late for me to run.

MY feet are wet waiting for Cecil.

I'm cold from standing in the early-morning dew waiting for the stepfather who left me a few months ago and never looked back. He ran out and probably never thinks about me.

It's cold and what I really want is to be in bed, covered up and warm. I want to hear my mom moving around in the kitchen and swearing when she drops something. I want to go to the park with my friends and eat hamburgers at The Loft.

I want to feel like I used to when it was just me,

Mom, and Cecil. Sometimes Cecil. Not the times he'd forget about me, or tell me to stay out of his business, or not think my nightmares were worth talking about . . .

I want to feel like I did when we woke up early and ran through the quiet city, just me and him. Then I want to feel warm and safe as we run into the house and Mom is there with juice and the kitchen is bright.

I want him to chase me, catch me, fall down with me, and do it all over again, like my dad used to do.

I want my dad, but he died when I was two . . .

Then I hear the foot sounds that I've heard for years coming at me, falling on the ground in soft thuds. I've heard those sounds so much, they're in my head. They're in my heart.

I want my dad.

I want my dad.

That's when I jump into the high grass to hide, and in about thirty seconds, Cecil has run on by.

He's not the one. This man that runs before the sun

is up and doesn't say good-bye or talk about the people he loves.

He's not the one.

I walk back into town, my head pounding with every step. The sky is pink by the time I get back to Overlook Street and Mrs. Pritchard. Garbagemen are out and the mist is lifting when I walk up the steps to the front porch, open the door, and walk toward the upstairs.

Somebody is sleeping on the couch. I can't see who it is 'cause they have a blanket covering their face. There's half a glass of lemonade on the table beside whoever, but I'm so tired, I keep on going.

I look in on Mrs. Pritchard and she's gone back to sleep. I don't want to wake her up, but I do.

"Mrs. Pritchard?" I say, standing in her doorway.

She sits up real slow. "Yes, Miss Bird?"

"I think it's time for me to go home, Mrs. Pritchard. It's time for me to go back."

"Hmmm. Well, I thought we might just talk about that today. But you beat me to it."

"I guess I did," I say, smiling into the shadowy bedroom that smells like lilacs.

Mrs. Pritchard drives me to the bus station after she fills me up with breakfast and tells me stories about her husband.

He was a Tuskegee Airman and he loved to fish. He also loved the way she drove his truck 'cause she always did it with her foot down, hard on the pedal. She still drives that way. And I swear she must have been going seventy right through town.

She double-parks at the Greyhound stop by the bank, sits with me until the bus pulls up, and hands me a big bag of food, but never tells me to be careful. Just good-bye and, "Your mom will be expecting you."

The bus starts moving before I get to my seat. By the time I've settled in the middle of the bus, she's gone. I can see the back of the truck flying down Decatur Street.

⊛

In a few hours the bus blows by the WELCOME TO TENNESSEE sign. I sink down in my seat and try to sleep. Now the only place I want to be is where I'm going.

❀ ANGELA JOHNSON, the author of novels, short stories, poetry, and picture books, is as acclaimed as she is versatile. A recipient of the prestigious MacArthur Fellowship, she has also won the Printz Award and the Coretta Scott King Award, and her books have appeared on the ALA Notable, Best Books for Young Adults, and Quick Picks lists. She lives in Kent, Ohio.